SKATEBOARD PARTY

•• THE CARVER CHRONICLES ••

— BOOK TWO —

SKATEBOARD PARTY

BY Karen English

ILLUSTRATED BY Laura Freeman

Houghton Mifflin Harcourt

Boston · New York

All rights reserved. Originally published in the United States in hardcover by
Clarion Books, an imprint of Houghton Mifflin Harcourt Publishing Company, 2014.

For information about permission to reproduce selections from this book, write to
trade.permissions@hmhco.com or to Permissions, Houghton Mifflin Harcourt Publishing
Company, 3 Park Avenue, 19th Floor, New York, New York 10016.

www.hmhco.com

The text was set in Napoleone Slab.
The illustrations were executed digitally.

The Library of Congress has cataloged the hardcover edition as follows
English, Karen.
Skateboard party / by Karen English ; illustrated by Laura Freeman.
p. cm — (The Carver chronicles ; book 2)
Summary: "Richard can't wait to show off his skills at a friend's skateboard
birthday party, but a note home from his teacher threatens to ruin his plans."
— Provided by publisher.
[1. Schools — Fiction. 2. Skateboarding — Fiction. 3. African Americans — Fiction.]
I. Freeman-Hines, Laura, illustrator. II. Title.
PZ7.E7232Sk 2014
[Fic] — dc23
2013048934

ISBN: 978-0-544-28306-0 hardcover
ISBN: 978-0-544-58226-2 paperback

Manufactured in the United States of America
DOC 10 9 8 7 6
4500624537

• Contents •

One
A Note from Ms. Shelby-Ortiz

Richard is watching the clock above the whiteboard. Four minutes until his weekend officially begins. Well, not technically, but in his mind. When the bell rings, that's the signal for freedom. He only has to endure waiting for everyone at his table to straighten up and look "ready to be dismissed." Those are Ms. Shelby-Ortiz's words. She's the teacher and she's really nice and he likes her a lot.

When his table is called, he will have to hold himself back from jumping up and running out of there. First, he must get up and push his chair under the desk and stand behind it like a soldier. Mouth zipped. Then, he'll have to walk in an "orderly fashion" to the line at the classroom door. He'll have to make sure he keeps his lips together and doesn't punch Ralph in the shoulder for fun. He'll have to make sure he doesn't make a fart sound with his hand in his armpit. He must try really hard not to pull one of Nikki's fat braids. It's truly difficult to be perfect.

He looks over at Gavin, his new best friend. Gavin can do all that being good stuff so easily. He doesn't even look tempted to jump around or pull a braid or give a punch. He makes it look easy to be good.

The bell rings. It sounds like music to Richard's ears. Ms. Shelby-Ortiz starts to look around. All the students are hurrying to put away their textbooks, load up their backpacks, check the floor around their desks, and then stand ramrod-straight behind their chairs. Richard is the best straight-as-a-ramrod stander at his table. He knows Ms. Shelby-Ortiz is going to compliment him. He can just hear the words: *I really love the way Richard is standing. He looks ready to be dismissed.* He waits for them. His table is the best, without a doubt. Ralph, at Table Four, is still picking up paper off the floor. Hah, hah.

Ms. Shelby-Ortiz begins her stroll. Walking slowly,

checking desks, looking at the floor ... "I like Table Three," she says.

Hooray — that's his table!

"Yes. They look all ready to line up."

Come on, Ms. Shelby-Ortiz ... More praise, please. Richard looks over at Gavin and smiles, but Gavin is busy looking straight ahead.

"Okay, Table Three. You may line up."

Richard tries hard not to shoot out from behind his desk and fast-walk to the door.

"Except Richard — I want you to be seated for now."

At first, he thinks he didn't hear correctly. Did Ms. Shelby-Ortiz tell him to be seated? Did he hear her right? The other three students at his table quietly walk to the door. Richard sits back down and looks around as Ms. Shelby-Ortiz dismisses the rest of the class, table by table.

When the last student walks out, she goes to her

desk and puts her grade book — the dreaded grade book — in the middle of it. She looks over at Richard, smiles, and says, "Come on over here, Richard, and have a seat."

He doesn't like the way the chair looks, facing Ms. Shelby-Ortiz's desk. It looks like the chair of a person guilty of something. He hopes this doesn't have anything to do with his accidentally not giving his part of the presentation about the habitat of the howler monkey last week. He was hoping she had just kind of forgotten about it.

Richard sits down and looks at his hands. Ms. Shelby-Ortiz settles into her chair. "We have a problem," she says.

Richard keeps looking down at his hands.

Ms. Shelby-Ortiz opens her grade book.

Uh-oh. Richard swallows. He doesn't like that grade book. He feels as if it contains a bunch of evidence against him. Bad spelling grades and test grades and things like that. He looks out the window and wishes he were one of the kids running for the bus or laughing and talking with friends.

"What happened to your part of the rainforest report? Weren't you supposed to turn that in last Friday?" Ms. Shelby asks.

Richard stares at his hands some more and thinks. The class had broken up into groups. Each group had chosen a rainforest animal. He was in Group Howler Monkey, which included Erik Castillo, Yolanda, and Nikki. Richard was supposed to do the habitat; Erik was supposed to do what the howler monkey preys on and what its predators are; and Nikki and Yolanda were doing the visual aids: charts and pictures, some drawn and some copied from books and stuff.

The day of the presentation, Richard had been home sick. Kind of. Well, truthfully, he'd only had the sniffles and he supposed he could have gone to school. Except that he'd kind of spent too much time playing video games and just generally goofing off in the days leading up to the presentation. By the time he got down to work, it was Sunday night and the report was due on Monday. And he really was a little bit sniffly.

Ms. Shelby-Ortiz let Group Howler Monkey delay their report until that Friday, and it did seem as though he had plenty of time to get it together, but Friday came really fast and Richard still wasn't ready. The group had to present their report without the part about the habitat of the howler monkey.

Ms. Shelby-Ortiz said she'd give him until Monday. Monday came really fast, too.

Now it's Friday and she clearly hasn't forgotten about the presentation. "I'm sorry, Richard," she says. "You've not been doing your best work in other areas as well." She runs her finger down her grade-book page and stops at his name. "Oh my," she says under her breath as she moves her finger across the page, stopping every few moments to *tsk-tsk* to herself. She turns a few more pages, finds his name again, then runs her finger across that one. Every once in a while she shakes her head slowly. And sadly. "These spelling grades are not good. And your math quizzes ... I know you can do better."

Richard looks down again but hears Ms. Shelby-Ortiz open her drawer. He glances up to see her with that scary pad in front of her, the one for requesting that a parent or guardian come in for a conference. She begins to write on it.

Quickly, Richard starts making some calculations. If he brings the note home that day and gives it to his parents, there goes his weekend. There goes Gregory Johnson's skateboard party next Saturday. There goes lounging around, watching TV and playing video games, and practicing his flat-ground Ollie, his favorite skateboard trick. And here comes a miserable weekend, with extra chores designed to make him learn responsibility and provide him with the opportunity to think about his bad choices. He doesn't want a weekend of chores and thinking about how he can do better. What kid would? No — it would be better to hold off on giving that note to his parents as loooong as possible. *Yeah,* he thinks. That's just what he's going to do.

● ● ●

"So that's what I'm going to do," he tells Gavin on the way home from school.

"But, Richard, why didn't you just do the report? Wouldn't that have been easier?"

"Yeah. And I meant to do it. I really did. But then I got busy, and before I knew it, it was Sunday night."

"But didn't Ms. S. give your group extra time? Why didn't you get it done then?"

"I know, I know. I meant to."

Gavin looks at him and shakes his head. "I hope that works for you."

Richard changes the subject. "Gregory Johnson's skateboard party is a week from Saturday, and wait till you see what I'm going to do! It's going to be awesome."

"What are you going to do?"

"It's a surprise. You'll see." He doesn't know why he's sounding so confident. He's planning on doing a flat-ground Ollie over a crate, which is really hard. He's never done one before. But he's got it down pat *without* a crate, so he should be able to do it over a crate, right? At least that's what he tells himself.

They part when they reach Fulton, Richard's street. Gavin goes on to his own street, Willow Avenue.

● ● ●

As soon as Richard walks through the front door, Darnell appears out of nowhere and gives him a punch on the arm. Darnell, who's in fifth grade, is always doing things like that. But Richard doesn't really care. It's Friday and it's going to be an awesome weekend. He tries to punch Darnell back, but his brother dances out of the way, laughs, and then runs upstairs. That's okay. He'll get Darnell — when he least expects it. They share the same room, so there will be plenty of opportunity.

Richard has two other brothers: Jamal, who's in seventh grade, and Roland, who's a ninth-grader.

They drive their mom nuts with all the noise and wrestling and play fighting and arguments over chores and video games. Sometimes she goes into her room to escape with a book just to "restore my sanity," as she puts it. Then it's great because it's just the guys — his dad included.

On Fridays during basketball season, Richard's mom retreats to her room with a book and Richard's dad orders an extra-large pizza. All the guys sit around and watch the game together and then shoot hoops in the driveway at halftime. Fridays are great. *Who needs to think about that dumb note from Ms. Shelby-Ortiz when you're in the middle of having a great time on a Friday night?*

wonders Richard. He thinks of the note, tucked away in his backpack, for a few seconds, but then he puts it right out of his mind. It's Friday night.

TWO
Cinnamon Crunch and Cream Puff Pursuits

The sun on his eyelids wakes Richard on Saturday morning. He opens one eye and stares at Darnell's sleeping face across the room in his own bed under the window. Darnell's mouth is hanging open and Richard can see a thin line of slobber going down the side of his cheek. Richard eases out of bed and stands, looking at his brother. There's a can of soda on the floor beside Darnell's bed. Their mother doesn't allow food or drinks in the bedroom, and Richard is torn between telling on Darnell and doing something funny as revenge for that punch in the arm—which still hurts, by the way.

He opts for the latter. But first he has to make his

morning trip to the bathroom. When he comes back, he creeps across the room and picks up the can. There's a little bit of soda still inside. He looks at Darnell. Now Darnell's mouth is closed and he has a frown on his face, as if he might be dreaming he's being chased by a big, growling dog. Richard chuckles to himself and positions the can just over Darnell's head. Slowly, he begins to tilt the can until the liquid is poised at the opening.

Darnell makes a smacking sound, as though he's dreaming of eating pancakes or fried chicken or something. Richard tilts the can a bit more until a tiny drop of soda falls onto Darnell's face. Darnell frowns again and bats at his face as if there's a fly giving him an annoying tickle. Richard nearly doubles over with silent laughter. He calms himself and then tilts the can little by little until another drop falls onto Darnell's chin.

Darnell grunts and scratches his chin. Richard has to dash out into the hall so he can laugh without being heard. Then he creeps back in with the can of soda. With a big grin, he pours the remaining liquid in the can onto Darnell's forehead.

Darnell sits straight up, blinking and looking around. His eyes settle on Richard and then the can. He throws the covers back and leaps out of the bed, yelling, "You're in for it!" But Richard is already out the door and hurrying down the stairs, with Darnell close on his heels. He feels his pajama top being jerked back and suddenly Richard is on his backside, trapped in a chokehold from behind. He begins to protest loudly while Darnell screams, "What's wrong? You started it — now I'm going to end it!"

Richard tries to pull Darnell's arms away. "Let go!" he shouts, hoping his mother will come get him out of this predicament as soon as possible.

Darnell is now digging his knuckle into Richard's shoulder. It's one of his specialty moves.

"Quit it!" Richard yells. *Where is Mom?* he thinks. "Get off of me!"

"Ah, you can't take it, can you?"

"It was only a little soda! I was only playing!"

Richard feels Darnell digging in more as he struggles to escape. He feels tears gathering. He wills them away. If Darnell sees that he's brought Richard to tears, Richard will be in for all-day teasing. "Let me go!" he screams even louder. Finally he hears the approach of his mother's slippers as they slap against the floor. She appears at the bottom of the stairs, looking up with squinted eyes.

Darnell drops his hands, releasing Richard. Their mother crosses her arms. "I know you're not causing this ruckus first thing Saturday morning when you  both know I've been volunteering all week at the food bank and I look forward to sitting at the table quietly with my coffee and the newspaper before all you knuckleheads get up and start with your commotion. I know I must be hearing things."

Now Richard sees his mother's nostrils flare and her eyes get even more squinty. That's her look just before she comes up with some awful punishment. He can sense Darnell's dread. This might even warrant cleaning out the garage with all those spider webs and bugs.

"If I hear this kind of commotion one more time, I'm going to find a way for you to rid yourselves of all that extra energy. Am I making myself clear?"

"Yes," they both say in small voices.

"What?" she says. "I didn't hear you."

"Yes!" they say, louder and in unison.

With that, their mother nods, turns on her heels, and goes back to the kitchen.

Darnell gives Richard a sneaky final punch.

Richard starts to say "I'm telling ..." but he stops himself and sighs heavily. He pulls himself to his feet and stomps up the stairs. Time to get his Saturday going. He needs to practice his flat-ground Ollie over a crate if he's going to show it off at Gregory Johnson's party. As he goes into the bathroom to wash his face and brush his teeth, he wonders what kind of birthday cake Gregory's going to have.

Of course, that's when Darnell gets out his own toothbrush to start brushing his teeth alongside Richard, spitting into the sink without turning on the water to rinse away the mess. Darnell knows Richard is squeamish, for some strange reason, about spit mixed with toothpaste. It almost makes him gag. Richard pushes at Darnell with the side of his body to get him out of the way. Darnell pushes back. It all has to be done silently lest they both wind up cleaning out the garage.

Finally, disgusted, Richard goes to his parents' bathroom. He has to be extra quiet because his father is still sleeping. It's only when he's tiptoeing past his snoring father that he remembers the note tucked away in his backpack. And again he pushes the thought of it out of his mind.

● ● ●

Everybody gets his own breakfast on Saturday mornings. Jamal and Roland are still asleep. They always sleep late on Saturdays. *Good,* Richard thinks. That means there should still be plenty of Cinnamon Crunch left for him and Darnell. Richard had just opened a new box the day before. There it is, sitting on top of the refrigerator. Tomorrow it will be almost gone, and it's not as though his mother will dash to the market to buy more just because they run out. She'll wait until it's time to go grocery shopping again, next week. Until then, the family will be down to those little packets of hot cereal—oatmeal or Cream of Wheat. Richard looks over his shoulder at the kitchen door. Looks like Darnell has gotten sidetracked by something.

Quickly, Richard opens the cabinet where his mother keeps all those plastic containers for storing food. He glances at the kitchen door again, gets the box of cereal off the refrigerator, and pours half of it into a plastic container. He puts the top back onto the container and then looks for a hiding place.

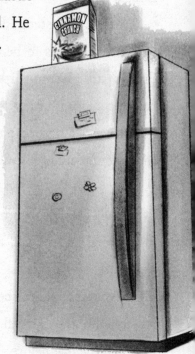

Suddenly he hears Darnell on the stairs. He glances around again and shoves the container into the oven just in time. Darnell comes into the kitchen yawning. Richard shakes some cereal into a bowl and hands the box to Darnell, trying to look innocent. Darnell shakes the box, frowning. He shrugs and fills a bowl, then puts the cereal box back on top of the fridge.

Just as they're sitting down at the table, Jamal comes in, also yawning. He doesn't speak — just goes to the refrigerator and gets the box of Cinnamon Crunch. He opens it and peers inside. "What? Who ate all the cereal? There's just some crumbs left!"

"I just have this one bowl," Darnell says.

"Me, too," Richard says, without looking up. He finishes wolfing down his cereal and brings the bowl to his lips to drink the milk.

"Mom just bought this box two days ago."

Richard shrugs and sets his bowl down.

Then they hear their mother's voice calling from the dining room, where she's cutting out coupons from last week's Sunday paper. "Don't you dare go into the cream puffs," she says. "They're for my book club meeting today."

All three boys say, "Cream puffs?"

Richard goes to the refrigerator, opens it, and sees a big pink box. He lifts the lid and there they are. Looks like at least a dozen. He swallows. He knows he's going to sneak one later when half the club members pass because of their diets or something. He just has to wait it out. He decides to go into the den and watch cartoons. Once he's sprawled on the couch, he thinks: *Ah, Saturday.*

After a while, he gets tired of cartoons and decides it's time to go out and practice the flat-ground Ollie before his mother comes up with a zillion chores for him to do. He needs to get it perfect so he's not nervous when it's time to show off at Gregory Johnson's party. He scoots out the back door to the driveway, grabs his skateboard leaning against the garage, and the crate next to it. His heart begins to beat fast. If his heart is beating fast now — while he's setting up at home — how will he feel at the skate park?

After executing two perfect Ollies in a row, he messes up the third. He misses his landing. *That's okay,* he tells himself. He just needs to practice. He's got a whole week to get it right. He's got until two o'clock next Saturday. He and Gavin plan to walk over to the park — where the party's going to be — together.

Richard thinks he feels a drop of rain. He looks up and sees dark clouds. Then the rain begins to fall. Richard considers doing one more flat-ground Ollie, but the rain is coming down a little harder. *I'll wait it out,* he thinks as he takes a seat on the top back-porch step. He sighs. Just his luck. What if it doesn't stop raining? It has to stop. If it doesn't, he'll practice the move in his mind.

So that's what he does. He sits on the top step and practices the move in his mind until he hears his mother open the back door. "What are you doing sitting out here in the rain?"

"I'm practicing a move in my mind for Gregory Johnson's birthday party at the park."

"You don't need to practice in the rain. The party's a week away. You've got plenty of time to practice."

Just my luck, Richard thinks. *Just my luck that it would start to rain.* He stays outside for a little longer, then decides he needs a cream puff. He needs a cream puff and a video game.

Inside, he peeks through the door that leads to the dining room and sees that the pink box has been moved to the dining room table. His mother's book club meeting has started in the living room, right next to the dining room. Several of the women have cream puffs on their paper plates. A really fat lady has two! Will Richard be able to sneak one cream puff out of that pink box without being seen? He listens to the women talking to one another. It doesn't seem as if the meeting has really started yet. It feels as though this is the refreshment part of the meeting. Then he hears someone with a commanding voice say, "Ladies, can I have your attention?"

While Richard imagines all eyes on that bossy-sounding woman, he tiptoes to the dining room table, opens the box, and plucks a cream puff out of it. He knows it's going to taste so good while he sits on his bed playing his new video game. For half a second he thinks of Ms. Shelby-Ortiz's note safely tucked away in his backpack.

He quickly thinks about the cream puff instead. No need to ruin a perfectly good Saturday afternoon.

But then later that night, when he's watching television with Darnell, Roland, and Jamal, the note pops into his head again. He almost gets up to retrieve it and give it to his mom, who right then is in the kitchen, talking on the telephone to her sister, his aunt Jen. Maybe his mom would be so busy talking that she'd sign it without really looking at it. But Richard decides that's not a good idea. He'll just give it to her at breakfast.

There doesn't seem to be a good time on Sunday at breakfast, or during the rest of the day. And Monday morning at breakfast doesn't seem to be the right moment either. His mother is having a good time laughing and talking with his father. *Why spoil the mood?* Richard thinks.

Later, when he's walking to school with Gavin, the note is still at the bottom of his backpack — right where he had put it on Friday.

Three
A Burned-Up Blob

As soon as Richard enters the classroom, he goes to his cubby and deposits his lunch. He unzips his backpack, gets his notebook, then takes out a couple of small racers and a wad of clay. He sees the note looking up at him. He slips the little cars and the clay into his pocket and goes to his desk. He's one of the kids who have to leave their backpacks in their cubbies. The students usually hang them on the backs of their chairs, but once Ms. Shelby-Ortiz decides you're a kid who's constantly going into your backpack for sneaky snacks or tiny toys, your backpack has to be left in your cubby. Richard hates leaving his. There are other kids who he *knows* are going into their backpacks for stuff all day long. Ms. Shelby-Ortiz just hasn't caught them.

He glances over his shoulder at his teacher. She's busy looking at some papers in her hand. He wonders if she's going to ask him for the signed note so she'll know when his parents are coming in for a conference to discuss how he isn't applying himself. He goes to his desk, takes out his morning journal, and looks at the board. The topic of the day is My Weekend There's a lot to write about, but Richard sighs heavily. That's just the problem. It's harder to get started when there's a lot to write about than when there's nothing to write about. When there's nothing much to put in his journal, he can make the words really big and write the same sentences in a couple of different ways each.

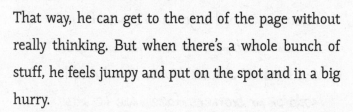

That way, he can get to the end of the page without really thinking. But when there's a whole bunch of stuff, he feels jumpy and put on the spot and in a big hurry.

He glances over at Ms. Shelby-Ortiz again. Now

she's looking at her plan book. All of his classmates are basically quiet and on task, as if they're tired from the weekend or something. Finally, Richard begins to write:

I had a fun weekend and a not fun weekend. First, I thot (I know I didn't spell that right but I don't want to ask anyone how to spell thot) I was going to practice this new move on my skateboard to show off at Gregery Johnsons party. But then it started to rain. But I got to play video games and I got a creem puf from my moms club meeting and that was good. And I played with my brothers and pored soda on my brothers face while he was asleep. That was real fun but then he woke up and started punching me and stuff. And I ate Cinamon Crunch for breakfast and then I hid some in the oven to eat later and I am going to eat it today after school.

Just then Ms. Shelby-Ortiz says, "Journals closed. Leave them in the upper corner of your desk. I will collect them and check them at recess. Please take your readers to your groups."

Everyone gets up and goes to their reading groups. Richard knows he's in the slow group, even though Ms. Shelby-Ortiz doesn't call it that. It's the group where she sits during oral reading. She "visits" the other groups while they're reading out loud to one another, but she mostly stays at the table where Richard sits. When he gets there today, Yolanda is already seated. She's a really slow reader. When she reads, it takes so long for her to get through one paragraph that Richard practically falls asleep. He doesn't know how Ms. Shelby-Ortiz can keep such a happy look on her face. He looks over at Gavin at the smart table. He knows Gavin is in the top reading group because they're all the time getting to do independent activities: writing skits, writing letters to a famous person from the past, rewriting the ending of their favorite book ...

Gavin wrote a letter to Davy Crockett. He asked him if he actually wrestled with a bear and what kind of wrestling moves he did — which Richard thought was a really good question.

After oral reading, the students take out their workbooks and answer a bunch of questions about what they just read. Ms. Shelby-Ortiz guides Richard's table through this, too. The whole time she's there, Richard can't tell if she's going to ask him about the note or not. He begins to hope she forgot. At the moment she's helping Yolanda and letting the rest of the class work on their own. Richard wishes he could get to the little cars in his desk. It would help if he could play a little bit while he works. He looks over at Gavin, who is busy writing his answers. Richard wishes he could sit by Gavin and get some of them from him.

"Richard," Ms. Shelby-Ortiz says.

Richard holds his breath. Here it comes.

"I'm sorry. I know you're working hard, but can you stop what you're doing and take the lunch count to the office?"

Whew! He'd forgotten that he's office monitor this week. He loves being office monitor. He loves getting out of class and walking down the hall and looking in other classrooms that have their doors open. He wishes he could be office monitor for the rest of the year. He takes his time.

When he returns, his classmates are busy putting away their readers and workbooks in preparation for recess. Wow! What luck. He hurries to his table and puts away his reader and workbook, pushes his chair forward, and stands behind it like a soldier. It's a beautiful sound when Ms. Shelby-Ortiz calls Table Three to line up first.

"You're lucky Ms. Shelby-Ortiz has forgotten," Gavin says to Richard on their way to the basketball court. Gavin is ball monitor this week. He shoots the basketball to Richard.

"Yeah," Richard agrees, and bounces the ball low all the way to the court. The day's starting off great.

● ● ●

Except later, after lunch and during math, which Richard kind of likes, Ms. Shelby-Ortiz says, "Richard, please come up here." She's sitting at her desk. There on the desk is her grade book. He hopes she doesn't start flipping through the pages again, looking for his name. She doesn't. She folds her hands and studies him closely. "I'm wondering if you have the note I gave you on Friday to give to your parents." She looks at him as if she already knows the answer.

Richard swallows nervously. He doesn't like the way Ms. Shelby-Ortiz is staring at him now, without saying anything. She's doing that waiting thing. "I forgot it at home," he says.

"Mmm."

Richard doesn't know what that means. Does it mean she doesn't believe him or does it mean that she *does* believe him?

"Okay," she says. "I'm going to be looking for it tomorrow. But if you don't bring it tomorrow, what do you think should be your consequences?"

He doesn't like it when Ms. Shelby-Ortiz makes them come up with their own consequences. He's always tempted to come up with something easy, like missing one recess or doing yard cleanup, which can be kind of fun. Walking around picking up paper can easily be turned into play, especially if you're working with a partner.

He sighs and says, "I have to miss recess?"

"That's a start, but I think you should miss morning *and* lunch recesses until I receive the note," she says, and smiles at him. "Do you think that's fair?"

This is the hard part. He has to say yes when he wants to say no. But he can't say no. Because it really is fair. "Yes, it's fair," Richard says in a low voice.

"Good," Ms. Shelby-Ortiz says. "I'm glad you see it my way. Now go over to the whiteboard and write 'Richard's note' in the bottom corner so I can see it first thing in the morning."

Richard walks to the whiteboard. He can feel the eyes of the class on him. He picks up the dry-erase marker and writes "Richard's note." It's kind of messy because the whiteboard is slippery and it's hard to control the marker. He returns to his seat and thinks about how he'll tell his parents about the note and the missed project.

● ● ●

Richard's mother had given permission for Gavin to come over after school to do homework, and Richard has been looking forward to doing a little bit of homework and a lot of playing video games. But as soon as Gavin and Richard walk through the back door of his house, he sees he has a new problem. Darnell and Jamal had dentist appointments, so they are already home with their mom. Roland had a half-day at school, so he's there in the kitchen as well. The only one who isn't standing at the kitchen table looking at the strange thing in the middle of it is their father.

Richard can't make out what it is. Gavin stares at it with his mouth hanging open. It appears to be a blob of plastic with some burned, brown, crunchy-looking stuff in it. His mother is giving Richard her squinty-eye look. "Look what I found in the oven," she says. "When we all got back from the dentist, I thought to myself, *Why don't I*

make my boys some chocolate chip cookies as a treat?
Everybody's been doing pretty good in school — no bad
reports — and keeping up with their chores at home.
So I turn on the oven to three hundred seventy-five
degrees. The phone rings and I'm talking to your Aunt
Jen for a while when I begin to smell this strange odor.
I get off the phone and run to the kitchen, thinking
something's on fire. I open the oven door and see this."
She points at the blob.

Richard looks at the blob again and then does a
double take. Suddenly he knows what it is. *Oh, no!* He
had forgotten all about putting the plastic container

of Cinnamon Crunch cereal in the oven to hide it from his brothers.

"Who did this?" his mother asks, looking at each of them to see who looks guilty.

"Wasn't me," Roland says. "I had to have a peanut butter and jelly sandwich for breakfast yesterday."

Everyone looks at Roland. He's suddenly gotten taller and skinnier — in just the past few months. Now he's on the basketball team at his school and he's really good.

"I didn't do it," Jamal says. "I was wondering why the box was nearly empty when you had just bought that cereal."

"I didn't do it either," Darnell says, looking right at Richard.

Richard looks away. But he can feel all eyes on him. Even Gavin's.

"Richard?" his mother says. "Did you do this?"

He glances up at her and knows he'd better tell the truth.

"I just wanted to put some away for later. And I didn't know where to put it, and ..."

"Stop right there," his mother says, raising her palm. "This is ridiculous. Look at my good plastic container."

Everyone looks at the melted blob again.

"You're going to replace that," she says. "It's coming out of this week's allowance. You can be sure."

Richard looks down. He'd had plans for his allowance. He and Gavin are saving up for new skateboards. Now Gavin will probably save enough first and Richard is going to have to see him on a super new skateboard while Richard is stuck using his old one.

"And forget about TV tonight. You need to work on getting some common sense." Richard's mom turns to Gavin and says, "I think it would be better if you come back another time. Richard's not up to having company today."

Richard looks over at Darnell and sees him smirking at him. Darnell loves to see Richard get into trouble.

Four
Memory *Not* Like an Elephant

When Richard enters the classroom the next morning, he looks quickly at Ms. Shelby-Ortiz. She's busy
talking to Mr. Beaumont from the other third grade
class. She doesn't even glance his way. He checks the
whiteboard. He sees the words he wrote there the
day before: *Richard's note*. Ms. Shelby-Ortiz probably
didn't even need him to write that. She probably has a
memory like an elephant. Richard looks around, surprised to see all the kids going about their business. It
always feels funny to be worried about something and
see everyone else acting happy-go-lucky. He'd meant
to give his mother the note. He really had. But after all
that trouble about the burned-up plastic container, he
didn't want to mess things up more.

Ms. Shelby-Ortiz moves to the front of the class, raises her hand, and puts her forefinger to her lips with the other hand. It's her signal for them to quiet down, be seated, and listen to what she has to say. It isn't long before all of the students notice and stop what they're doing to give her their undivided attention.

Richard looks past her at his name on the board. Maybe he can accidentally-on-purpose erase it. Maybe Ms. Shelby-Ortiz will be so busy that she won't remember it was there.

"Class, I have good news," she says, bringing her arm down. "Mr. Beaumont's class has been working on oral language. They've broken into groups and have written their own skits! They want to perform one for us this morning." She looks around. "How many of you would like that?"

For a moment there's a lot of "Yeah, yeah"s and other unruly noises. Ms. Shelby-Ortiz has to put her forefinger to her mouth again and look around until everyone settles down.

As soon as she says, "I love Table Three. Look how they all have their hands folded," the rest of the students follow suit and fold their hands. Ms. Shelby-Ortiz goes to the door and opens it, and Arthur Wang, Angela Martin, Myrella Hernandez, and Dyamond Taylor walk in looking as though they're about to burst out laughing. Myrella and Arthur have little white index cards in their hands.

Hmm, Richard thinks. *They probably haven't memorized their lines very good.*

The four students stand bunched in front of the whiteboard. They start talking in low voices among themselves.

Wow, they should have rehearsed more, Richard thinks.

Dyamond Taylor steps forward and says, "Today we're going to perform a skit we wrote entitled 'The Boy Who Lost His Lunch Money.'"

Richard feels a little laugh coming on. He has to pull in his lips to suppress it. He hears some giggles from Table Two. Now Arthur steps forward and pulls his pockets inside out. "Oh, no!" he says. "I lost my lunch money. Oh, no, what am I going to do?" He looks over at Myrella, who's looking at her index card.

It takes a long time for her to finally say, "Hi, Billy. What's wrong?" Richard hears snickers from behind him. He glances around. Deja is passing Nikki a note in that secret way that everybody already knows about. Deja folds the note into a tiny square, places it in the marker basket in the middle of the table, and then coughs. That's the signal. Nikki takes the note out of the basket, puts it on her lap, and reads it. Richard wonders what it says.

He looks at Yolanda yawning, and Carlos whispering to Ralph. But Gavin is just looking at the performers politely. He doesn't seem like he's about to laugh. He's just sitting there, watching.

Arthur looks at his card. "I lost my lunch money."

There's a long pause where Myrella just stares at him. Then Myrella says, "Oh, no, what are you going to do?"

Arthur looks at his card again. He squints at his writing. The class waits. At last he says, "I don't know."

Now Richard can hear Deja and Rosario giggling quietly. Ms. Shelby-Ortiz gives them a look and they stop. *This is not good,* Richard thinks. *They should have rehearsed.* Eventually Dyamond Taylor and Angela Martin make their entrance. They know their parts but their voices don't sound natural to Richard. They're speaking too slowly and in a tone that makes them sound like robots. Everyone finally helps Arthur retrace his steps. When he sees his pretend money on the ground, he reaches down and picks it up and puts it in his pocket. "Thank you for helping me find my lunch money," he practically shouts. The three girls just stand around looking at him, then Angela Martin starts cheering and Dyamond and Myrella join in. Then they stop abruptly. Richard doesn't know if that's the end or not, and neither does the rest of the class. Everyone waits in silence for a few seconds.

Then Ms. Shelby-Ortiz starts clapping and her students follow suit. "Thank you," she says. "Thank you so much. Class, wasn't that just wonderful?"

"Yes, Ms. Shelby-Ortiz," the class says, though they don't sound very enthusiastic. But there is one super great thing about the skit. When the four students file out, Richard sees that there's a smudge on the whiteboard where his name was written. One of them must have backed up into it and nearly wiped it away.

He looks over at Ms. Shelby-Ortiz, wondering if she'll notice the smudge and remember that "Richard's note" had been written there. He has an idea. Ms. Shelby-Ortiz tells the class to take out their morning journals and write about the importance of cooperation. That seems to be what the skit was about. Richard frowns. He knows he'll be staring at a blank page while he struggles to come up with something. Anything.

He thinks about cooperation for a bit. Then he takes a couple of old papers out of his desk that need to go into the recycle box. He doesn't have to get permission to put papers in the recycle box. No one does, because

his teacher wants to encourage the kids to recycle. Richard eases out of his seat — he doesn't want to draw attention to himself — and heads to the recycle box by way of the whiteboard. He slows as he passes his name and erases the smudge with his elbow. He looks back over his shoulder. *Problem solved,* he thinks as he deposits his papers and returns to his table. No one has noticed, except maybe Gavin, who is giving him a funny look.

● ● ●

"You didn't get your note signed, did you?" Gavin asks as they walk home.

"I'm going to get it signed," Richard answers. "By tomorrow."

Gavin is silent, but Richard can tell he doesn't believe him. "I think you're going to get in big trouble," Gavin says after a moment. "Danielle did the same thing. She had a note about all this missing homework, but she hid the note under her mattress because she wanted to go to her friend's slumber party. My mother found it when she went to change the sheets and boy, did Danielle get in trouble."

Sometimes Gavin can be a goody-goody, Richard thinks. He doesn't like him as much then, because it seems as if he's judging Richard, and that doesn't feel very good.

Gavin shakes his head slowly. "Richard, it would have been easier to just do the report."

"You've already told me that," Richard says. He hopes that's the end of it.

● ● ●

"Did you have a rainforest project you were supposed to do?" his mother asks as she passes a dish of green beans to his father. They're all at the kitchen table eating dinner. Roland just keeps on eating, but Darnell and Jamal look over at him. Darnell has a little smirk on his face.

"Huh?" Richard says.

"When I was going through your jeans pockets this afternoon before putting them in the washing machine, I found a paper on a rainforest project your class had to do. It had suggestions for animals and a kind of chart for getting things done so you'd be able to turn it in on time, et cetera, et cetera." She stops and stares at him, waiting.

His father has turned his way, also. Waiting.

Richard feels as if a hole is opening up and he's about to fall into it. Especially when he says, "Uh, yeah, but Ms. Shelby-Ortiz gave us more time." It's a big fib. He feels his face get warm.

His mother doesn't say anything for a few seconds. She just looks at him. Finally she says, "She did?"

The hole is getting deeper. "Uh-huh," Richard says quietly. He wonders if things can get any worse.

● ● ●

They do. Later, Darnell gets in on it. "What's this?" he says when Richard brings his plate to the sink. It's

Darnell's night to do dishes. "Look what I found in your backpack." Darnell flashes a big smile.

Richard recognizes the note immediately. Just what he needs . . . "What were you doing in my backpack?"

"Getting *my* ruler. The one I lent you last week for that math homework you had where you had to measure three things in our room. The ruler you never gave back to me."

"I need that," Richard says under his breath while reaching for the note.

"Not so fast, little brother," Darnell replies, snatching it back. He tucks it into his jeans pocket. "Whatcha gonna do for me in return?"

"You weren't supposed to be going through my things," Richard says.

"I was getting *my* ruler. I have a right to go through your stuff to get *my stuff.* Now, I could give this to Mom, or we could make a trade."

"What kind of trade?" Richard asks. He already knows this is not going to be good.

Darnell makes a sweeping motion toward the sink full of dirty dishes. "They're all yours."

"What? That's not fair."

"Would you rather do my dishes or have me give Mom this note?"

With that, Darnell tosses the sponge into the sink. Richard reaches for the note but Darnell jerks it away. "You'll get it . . . when I decide to give it to you."

● ● ●

The whole time Richard is rinsing plates and glasses and putting everything in the dishwasher where it can fit, then putting away the food, cleaning the stove, scrubbing the pots and pans, drying them, putting them away, and sweeping the floor as their mother always insists they do, he's thinking of what Gavin told him: *It would have been easier to just do the report.*

Five
The Jig Is Up

As soon as the class settles down the next day with their morning journals in front of them, Ms. Shelby-Ortiz walks up to Richard's desk, stands over him with her arms crossed, and says, "Where's your signed note, Richard? The one you were supposed to give to me yesterday?"

Richard can feel everyone looking at him. For some strange reason, he finds himself getting up out of his seat and going to his cubby. He retrieves his backpack, unzips it, and starts rummaging around as if he's searching for the signed note. The whole time he's doing this, he knows how stupid it looks. Some of the kids start laughing, until Ms. Shelby-Ortiz turns to give them her famous penetrating stare.

He rummages and rummages. Finally he says, "Uh, I think I left it at home."

"Yeah, *right*," Ralph calls out. Ms. Shelby-Ortiz has talked to the class about having low impulse control and doing stuff without thinking. *That's Ralph,* Richard thinks. *He's got a bad case of low impulse control.* Ms. Shelby-Ortiz turns to Ralph now.

"Did anyone ask your opinion?" she says calmly.

"No," Ralph says quietly.

"Then why are you giving it?"

Ralph looks down and the attention shifts back to Richard. He can see a smirk on Antonia's stuck-up face, and Rosario is covering her mouth, but he can see her shoulders shaking a little as she laughs.

"Come with me, Richard." Ms. Shelby-Ortiz leads him out into the hall. Richard knows that this is to give him privacy when she issues the consequences of his behavior. As soon as they're outside the classroom door, she says, "We both know you haven't given the note to your parents, don't we?" Richard looks down at the floor. His face feels warm. "This is what's going to happen: There will be no recess until I get that note —

signed by one of your parents — in my hand. That's morning and lunch recesses. Just as we discussed on Monday."

Richard continues staring at his feet. He waits for the rest of the consequences, because he knows there are more.

"And," she goes on, "if I don't get that note in my hand by tomorrow morning, I will be making a phone call to your parents either at your home or at their places of work."

Richard swallows. He knows Ms. Shelby-Ortiz means business. If she calls his dad at work or his mom at the food bank, he'll be put on punishment for *life*. Or something just as bad. He swallows again.

"Do you think that's fair?"

He hates when she asks that question. It usually *is* fair, but that's not the point. The point is the punishment he is sure to receive from his parents. He's painted into a corner. Might

as well give up. This playing-around-with-the-note hasn't been worth it. He sighs and follows Ms. Shelby-Ortiz back into the classroom. He can feel his classmates' curiosity as almost all eyes follow him to his seat. *There goes Gregory Johnson's birthday party at the skate park. There goes every fun thing in the world.*

● ● ●

Richard is filled with dread on the walk home. "Maybe it won't be so bad," Gavin offers.

"It's going to be bad," Richard says.

"But you're giving them the note without Ms. Shelby-Ortiz having to call them — at work."

"The note is dated last Friday, Gavin."

"Oh, right."

They're quiet. Richard knows Gavin is probably thinking, *I told you so*. But at least Gavin doesn't say it. They part when they reach Fulton, and Gavin walks on to his street. Richard looks at his house. He starts for it as if he's heading to prison. Not a good feeling.

● ● ●

"What's the problem?" Richard's mom asks at the dinner table. "Why are you picking at your food? You love lamb chops and mashed potatoes."

Darnell glances up from gnawing on what's left of his lamb chop. He looks at Richard's untouched food. Richard knows Darnell would like to snatch it off his plate.

"Use your knife and fork, Darnell," Richard's mom says. "And for Pete's sake, wipe your mouth — and not with the back of your hand." Darnell picks up his napkin and pats his mouth daintily, causing Jamal and Roland to break out laughing. Richard's sour expression remains.

"What's with you?" Roland asks.

"Nothin'."

His father turns his attention to Richard. "Yeah, what's going on? Why are you looking so down?"

"Can I have that lamb chop?" Darnell asks.

Richard moves his plate closer to his chest.

"No, you may not," Richard's mom says. She turns to Richard. "What's going on, Richard?"

"I have a note."

"A note?"

"From Ms. Shelby-Ortiz."

His mother and his father glance at each other.

"What is this about?" his father asks.

"Where's the note?" his mother asks.

"Darnell has it." Now all eyes turn to Darnell.

"Why does Darnell have it?" his mother asks.

"He found it in my backpack. That's why I had to do his dishes last night. So he wouldn't tell you about it."

Darnell squirms in his seat. "I was just joking."

"You mean to tell me you were blackmailing your brother? You owe him his night of dishes," his mother says.

"That's not fair," Darnell protests.

"Too bad," his father says. "Go get the note."

When Darnell comes back, Jamal says, "Can he do my dishes, too?"

His mother gives Jamal a look and he goes back to his mashed potatoes. Darnell places the note in her hands. She reads it. "I can't believe this. You let that rainforest project due date come and go, and you lied to me about it? You didn't even bother to do it?"

Now his mother's eyes have squinted down to slits. Richard doesn't like that face. It's a bad-news look. He glances over at his father. His dad is sitting back in his chair with his arms folded. Not a good look either.

"Check this out, Bill," Richard's mom says, passing him the slip of paper. "He got this note last Friday."

Richard wishes he could shrink so small, he'd disappear. Roland is chuckling under his breath and nudging Jamal with his elbow. Everyone is enjoying the show. Especially Darnell, it seems to Richard. *He* would probably enjoy it more if he didn't have *my* dishes to wash, Richard thinks.

"Your father and I are going to discuss this after dinner. Then we'll let you know what your consequences are going to be."

There was that word again. *Consequences.* Richard is beginning to hate that word.

● ● ●

It's hard to concentrate on his math homework. He's been reading the same word problem over and over. Richard imagines his mom and dad sitting in the dining room, beneath his bedroom, with their heads together, discussing his punishment. No wonder he can't concentrate on the word problem.

If a car is going 50 miles an hour, how many
hours does it take to get to the next town 200
miles away?

He knows it's a simple problem and he knows Ms. Shelby-Ortiz has gone over similar problems with the class, but he just can't concentrate. He decides to go on to the next one.

Jamie has 3 dollars and 50 cents. He needs
to buy school supplies. Pencils are 1 dime
each and notebooks are 2 dollars. Does he
have enough money to buy 1 notebook and
5 pencils? If so, how much change should he
receive?

Richard looks up to see Roland standing in the doorway, leaning on the doorjamb with his arms crossed. "Word of advice, little brother — because I've been there. Never think you can get away with anything. Most of the time you get caught and then it's worse." He smiles. "Got it?"

"Yeah," Richard says. He's got it, for now.

Just then, Jamal comes bounding up the stairs. He sticks his head into the room. "Mom wants you!" he says, seeming happy to be the one to deliver the summons.

His mother and father are both sitting in the dining room with their hands on the table and fingers laced. They look like the judges on those court shows on TV. Not good.

Richard looks down at his feet.

"Well, first of all, forget about Gregory Johnson's skateboard party."

Richard swallows. He struggles to keep his mouth from turning down.

"Forget about television and video games for the next ten days. Forget about going to friends' houses after school. Forget about making less than one hundred percent on next Friday's spelling test. Let me give you some advice: This is the time to really mind your p's and q's." His mother turns to his father. "Did I leave anything out?"

"Mmm," he says. "Dessert? No dessert for ten days."

That's not so bad, Richard thinks. They almost never have dessert. Everyone is on his own with after-dinner treats. So he'll have to do without cookies and ice cream and stuff like that for a while. Maybe he can buy some candy after school and keep it in his backpack. But 100 percent on next Friday's spelling test? He doesn't know about that one.

"Now, what should happen if we catch you, say, sneaking some candy into the house?" his father asks.

Richard looks up quickly. Is his father reading his mind? Richard shrugs slowly.

"Simple," his father says. "You get another week."

No candy, Richard thinks. *And no TV and no skateboard party. And I have to mind my p's and q's. This is going to be awful.*

"One more thing," his mother says. "We'll be meeting with your teacher on Friday to discuss how we can work together to keep you on course."

Richard feels as if a big weight has settled in his stomach, permanently.

"Oh, and don't think you don't have to do your part of the rainforest presentation. We want that done by next Friday."

● ● ●

"What happened?" Darnell asks as soon as Richard walks through the bedroom door. Darnell has finished the dishes and is sitting at his own desk.

Richard rolls his eyes. He's not going to give his brother a thrill recounting all the things that he's not going to be able to do. He sits down at his desk and looks at that stupid math problem about the car. He could ask Darnell, but he doesn't want Darnell to think he's dumb.

Six
Life on the Bench

So what's going to happen?" Gavin asks on the way to school the next day. Richard has told him a little about the night before.

"My parents are coming in for a conference tomorrow. And I can't do nothin' for the next ten days."

"Ten days from yesterday or ten days from today?"

Richard sighs. Only Gavin would ask that. "Ten days from yesterday," he says.

"Well, you got one day over with."

"And I really have to mind my p's and q's."

"What are p's and q's?"

"That's when you have to be real careful and do everything just right," Richard explains.

"Oh, you can do that," Gavin says.

"But I can't go to the party on Saturday. And I had a big surprise that I've been working on." *Well, not the jumping-over-the-crate part,* Richard thinks. *Yet.* "And I wanted everyone to see it."

Gavin doesn't seem to have an answer for that one.

"And I have to do the best I can on the spelling test tomorrow and get a hundred on *next* week's test."

"Wow," Gavin says. "At least it's not tomorrow's test. At least you get to have some time to really study."

"And my parents are giving me till next Friday to do that howler monkey thing, too." Richard sighs, feeling weary already.

● ● ●

As soon as Richard enters the classroom, he walks over to Ms. Shelby-Ortiz and hands her the signed note along with the note of apology his mother made him write. Ms. Shelby-Ortiz opens the first note and nods. "What's this?" she asks, holding up the second note.

"It's an apology," Richard says quietly.

Ms. Shelby-Ortiz brightens. "How nice of you, Richard. I'm looking forward to reading it and to talking to your parents tomorrow after school as well. I have a lot to go over with them."

Can anything sound worse? wonders Richard as he reaches his table. His teacher has a lot to go over with his parents about him? She's probably going to show them that grade book of hers. He can just imagine her flipping it open in front of his mother and father and running her finger down the page until she gets to his name. He can see her running her finger across the row of not-so-good grades, then turning the book toward his parents so they can get a look.

He slumps down in his seat just at the thought of it.

At recess, all the boys are talking about Gregory Johnson's upcoming party, so Richard decides to sit on a bench and think. The only reason he got invited was because he's Darnell's little brother. Gavin was given a thumbs-up because Darnell asked Gregory Johnson if he could come. Now Gavin is going to the skateboard party and Richard isn't. Somehow that doesn't seem fair. If Gavin is a true friend, he'll tell Richard that he has decided not to go. That he is going to come over to his house on Saturday instead and help him do the extra chores Richard's mom has come up with to keep him busy.

But Gavin doesn't offer anything, and now he runs over to the basketball court, not even really paying attention as Richard slinks over to the benches. No one seems to notice him. Calvin Vickers, who's been benched most of the week, doesn't even look over. Richard sits with his elbows propped on the table behind him and a glum look on his face while everyone is playing away as if he isn't there.

Oh, no, he thinks. *Here comes Harper.* It's just his luck that Harper is benched, too. Harper is a big bully in Darnell's class and some say he repeated the fourth grade. Or was it the third grade? Whatever the case, he's way bigger than everyone else, and he's usually benched two or three days out of the week.

Harper plops down next to Richard — even though there are plenty of other places to sit.

"What's with you? You benched, too?" he asks in his newly deepening voice. If he hadn't been held back, he'd be in sixth grade — middle school.

"No," Richard says.

"Why you sittin' over here, then?"

"I don't feel like playing basketball."

"You could play something else," he says.

"No, our area is basketball this week."

"So? You don't have to play in your area."

"I don't want to get in trouble."

Harper *tsk*s and then chuckles. He looks over at Miss Campbell, the new yard lady. She's the crossing guard, too. "She wouldn't notice. She's new and she hasn't learned who's who yet."

"I don't feel like playing anything today."

"How come?" Harper looks puzzled.

"I just don't."

Harper stares at him for a moment. Then he gets up and moves over next to Calvin Vickers. Richard breathes a sigh of relief.

● ● ●

"Why were you sitting on the bench?" Gavin asks while

they're in line waiting for Ms. Shelby-Ortiz to lead them back to class.

"I didn't feel like playing."

"Why?"

"Cuz."

Gavin shrugs and doesn't ask anything more. He's not pressing him for an explanation. Richard doesn't like that. But then Ms. Shelby-Ortiz walks up and it's time for everyone to stand like a soldier and keep their mouth closed.

● ● ●

As soon as they leave Carver Elementary School at the end of the day, Gavin says, "I'm getting me a new skateboard. I finally have enough saved. Wait until you see it at the skateboard party on ..." His voice dies away and he looks embarrassed.

"Did you forget I'm on punishment?" Richard asks.

"Sorry."

"You know you wouldn't even be going if it wasn't for me."

"I know that."

They are quiet for a while until Richard says, "So you're still going?"

They're nearing the point on Marin Street where they have to decide if they want to go to Mr. Delvecchio's store for a snack or go straight to Fulton toward Richard's house.

"You want to get some chips at Mr. D.'s?" Gavin asks.

"You didn't answer my question."

"I want to go," Gavin says in a quiet voice.

"Well, go," Richard says. "Nobody's stopping you." He keeps walking in the direction of his street, and Gavin follows. When Richard turns down Fulton and Gavin starts heading to Willow Avenue, Richard doesn't say another word. He knows he should wave goodbye, but he doesn't.

● ● ●

Richard takes the house key on a string from around his neck, unlocks the back door, and sees a note his mother left on the refrigerator as soon as he walks into the kitchen. His mom is at her volunteer job at the food bank downtown. She usually takes Thursdays off. The note reads:

Richard,
After you get your snack, take Miss Ida's trash cans to the curb. She sprained her ankle. Then I want you to sweep out the garage and knock down the spider webs. Next, weed the vegetable garden and water it. Remember, NO TELEVISION or VIDEO GAMES! Darnell has Homework Club and Roland has basketball practice, but Jamal should be home on time. Have him call my cell as soon as he gets home. Tell Jamal to do his homework before doing anything else.

Richard inhales deeply and lets out the longest breath he can muster. He opens the refrigerator door and stares inside for a while. Nothing. Nothing he can just reach for and shove into his mouth. He goes to the cabinets above the counter, throws them open. *Hmm ...* There are graham crackers and peanut butter. That will have to do.

Once Richard has fixed his snack and sat down to eat, Jamal pushes through the swinging door. He chuckles to himself when he sees Richard just about to take his first bite. "What's that?" he says, pointing toward the kitchen window.

Richard turns. "What?" he says. He sees nothing out the kitchen window but the old Chinese elm and the tire swing no one has used in a while.

When he turns back around, Jamal has disappeared and so have his peanut butter graham crackers. Richard sighs and gets the peanut butter and crackers down and starts all over. He won't fall for that trick again. At least not any time soon.

After he's taken Miss Ida's trash cans to the curb, swept the garage, knocked down the yucky spider webs, and weeded the garden, Richard uncoils the hose that's hooked to the faucet on the side of the house and waters the vegetables way longer than necessary. He dreads going into the house, knowing that finishing his homework does not mean he can relax in front of the television or with a video game. His only option after homework and chores is just to fool around — whatever that means.

Seven
And There Will Be Consequences

Richard isn't happy to see Friday come. Not only is it the day of his parents' conference with his teacher, but Friday is next to Saturday, so it reminds him that he won't be going to Gregory Johnson's skateboard party. He notices that Gavin is careful not to say a word about it. When some of the bigger boys invade their basketball court at recess and start talking about the party, Gavin doesn't join in. It seems as if he's being quiet for Richard's sake.

As they put their lunches in their cubbies, Gavin tells him about a movie he saw the night before on television. But then he stops suddenly, probably remembering that Richard is on TV punishment. They part ways to go to their separate tables. The air feels somber.

● ● ●

Since the parent conference is scheduled for right after dismissal, Richard wishes the school day could go on forever, but he'd also like to get the horrible meeting over with at the same time. During math, while everyone is studying for the multiplication-facts quiz (sixes, sevens, and eights), he glances up from his facts sheet and looks around. He wishes he were someone else. He'd even be Calvin Vickers right about now. Calvin's been benched for five days for being caught with mancala pieces in his pocket.

It was Carlos who'd accused him during a ten-minute free-time period right before dismissal on Tuesday. Ms. Shelby-Ortiz sometimes lets kids who have finished *all* of their work have a little bit of free time at the end of the school day.

"Ms. Shelby-Ortiz, how come we don't have half of the mancala pieces?" Chi Chi had called out, without raising her hand and waiting to be recognized. Ms.

Shelby-Ortiz left her desk and went over to the game table to investigate.

"Hmm," she said, frowning.

"I know what's been happening," Carlos announced. "I saw Calvin Vickers putting some in his pocket this morning when we were at the game table working on our skit."

Ms. Shelby-Ortiz had been so impressed with Mr. Beaumont's idea to have his students write skits that she was having her class do the same.

"You know you should not make accusations lightly, Carlos."

Carlos had just stared at Ms. Shelby-Ortiz, probably trying to decide what that meant.

"I saw him, too, Ms. Shelby-Ortiz," Ralph called out. "They're in his pockets. Check his pockets."

Ms. Shelby-Ortiz looked as if she didn't really want to, but she called Calvin over to her desk and asked him to turn his pockets inside out.

Calvin stood there before her as if he didn't know what to do. "But I didn't take no mancala pieces," he said, in a guilty voice. Ms. Shelby-Ortiz didn't say anything. She just waited.

Finally, Calvin reached into his pocket and pulled out three shiny glass pieces, each with a swirl of color inside. He dropped them into her waiting hand. "Is that all?" Ms. Shelby-Ortiz asked.

He reached into his other pocket, pulled out two pieces, and dropped them into her hand. She looked at the five pieces. "That's all, Ms. Shelby-Ortiz. For real," Calvin said.

She meted out his consequences then — benched for the next five days — and told him to return to his seat.

Richard looks over at Calvin now, wondering what makes people take things that don't belong to them. What are they thinking while they're doing something like that? Still, right then, he wouldn't mind trading places with Calvin Vickers — at least until the day is over.

● ● ●

"Come in, come in," Ms. Shelby-Ortiz tells Richard's mother and father. He'd spotted them waiting in the hall through the classroom door's window. They hadn't been saying anything to each other. They were just standing there.

"Please, sit down," Ms. Shelby-Ortiz says. She's put three chairs in front of her desk. A chair for each of them. "Richard, you sit down as well."

If only he could run away. He takes the seat between his parents and looks down. Ms. Shelby-Ortiz begins by telling them what a nice, polite boy Richard is. And though she feels he hasn't been applying himself, she had still been surprised that he "blew off" his rainforest project.

Richard doesn't like her use of the term "blew off." It makes him sound extra irresponsible. When she says it, both his mother and his father turn to look at him. He feels himself shrink down to the size of a puppy.

"What happened, Richard?" his mother asks.

He'd known she was going to ask that. "I don't know," he says. Because right then he really doesn't know.

"That's not an answer," his father says.

Richard feels himself shrink down to the size of a mouse.

Ms. Shelby-Ortiz opens her grade book then and angles it so they can get a good look while she runs her finger along his row of grades. Now Richard is the size of a ladybug.

● ● ●

All the way to the car, Richard has to hear his mother say, "I don't *believe* it! What are you doing in that class? I'm mortified!"

"We're going to get to the bottom of this," his father says. "And there will be consequences."

More consequences? wonders Richard.

On the way home, as if she can't bear to wait until they get there, his mother lists the new consequences tacked on to the old.

● ● ●

1. Richard has to mind his p's and q's and still can't do everything they discussed previously: watch TV, play video games, go to Gregory Johnson's skateboard party on Saturday. He must get 100 percent on his spelling test next

Friday. Plus, he has to complete his part of the rainforest project and present it to the class next Friday.

2. Richard is to show his homework journal to his mother every evening. Ms. Shelby-Ortiz has promised to occasionally email his assignments to his mother, so everything had better match. He will be benched from recess through the next week so he can keep on top of all of his assignments.

3. Even when he gets off TV and video game punishment, Richard must read one chapter in a book of his choosing and summarize the

chapter in complete sentences and legible handwriting every night.

This is a nightmare, he thinks.

And that's just for starters. There might be some more stuff she can think up. Richard knows his father's onboard because he keeps nodding slowly the whole time his mother is talking.

As soon as Richard walks into the house, Darnell sidles over to him. "What happened?" he asks, looking a little too excited for Richard's liking. Richard just walks past him, up the stairs to get started on his homework — and to think about his woes.

Later, after dinner, Richard has to sit up in his room while his father and his three brothers are whooping and hollering over the basketball game on television. Soon it's halftime and Jamal, Darnell, Roland, and his dad go out to the driveway to shoot hoops. Richard lies on his bed and tosses his balled socks up in the air — something he learned from Gavin. It's not so bad — tossing and catching, tossing and catching.

He stops when he hears a knock on the door. "Come in," he says.

It's his mother with a slice of pie on a plate. "I thought you might want this last piece of apple pie," she says, and he knows she's feeling a bit sorry for him.

"Thanks," he says. He doesn't dare mention the no-dessert consequence.

She looks at his book, *Henry Huggins,* lying open and face-down on the floor beside his bed. "Don't forget what I said about reading a chapter a day," she says before she turns and closes the door behind her.

Richard sighs and picks up the book. He's read only three pages so far.

Eight
Skateboard Party

Richard's dreaming of a marching-band guy banging on one of those big drums he has strapped to his chest. Richard hears it banging right in his ear. He opens one eye. Darnell is still asleep. *Why do I always wake up before any of my brothers,* Richard wonders. He's always up and raring to go way before anyone else. It can be lonely.

Suddenly there's a big crack of thunder and a flash of lightning that brightens the room. He jumps and looks over at Darnell. Darnell hasn't stirred. *What's wrong with that guy?*

Richard eases out of bed and goes to the window just as rain begins to pour from the sky. It's the most

beautiful sight he's ever seen. It's a full rainstorm. Not just a drizzle. *Awesome!*

"Oh, no," Darnell says, sitting up in bed and looking out the window. "Oh, no. That can't be rain."

Richard tries not to smile. He has to pull in his lips to avoid breaking out in a huge grin.

"Bet you're happy," Darnell says with a sneer.

● ● ●

Later in the morning, while Richard is loading the dishwasher with the breakfast dishes and still trying to keep from grinning, the phone rings. He can hear a little bit of his mother's side of the conversation because she's standing in the hall. He turns the water off and tiptoes to the kitchen door. "Uh-huh. Oh . . . I so understand." As soon as she hangs up, Richard hurries back to the sink.

"Where's Darnell?" his mother asks as she comes through the door. Before Richard can answer, she goes back into the hall and calls up the stairs. "Darnell, come down here, please."

She explains within Richard's hearing that there's not going to be a skateboard party that day. The rain is supposed to go on all afternoon. But the party is not completely canceled. A dry spell is due to arrive early in the week, so the party has been postponed until the next Saturday.

Hooray! Richard screams in his mind. As soon as he closes the door to the dishwasher, he runs out into the backyard and dances around in the rain.

"Yes! Yes!" he yells, spinning and twirling and

getting wet. All he has to do is mind his p's and q's for the rest of the week — which he plans to do. And get that rainforest stuff done and study for his spelling test. He throws his head back and opens his mouth to catch some rainwater.

"Richard, what are you doing?"

Richard looks over his shoulder to see his mother

standing on the back porch with her hands on her hips.

"I'm celebrating!" Richard says. "I'm celebrating that I'm not going to miss the skateboard party!"

"Well, you're not out of the woods yet, buddy boy. You need to come in out of the rain and get started on that report!"

That's fine with Richard. He realizes it's cold out in his backyard. He's done enough celebrating.

● ● ●

Richard's dad is letting him use his computer. Richard has already put "howler monkey" in the search box. Now he has to figure out what information he needs to print out. His father is also taking him to the library in the afternoon so he can get two books to use as sources. Ms. Shelby-Ortiz doesn't let kids just copy a bunch of stuff off the Internet. *That's the hard part,* Richard thinks, *reading stuff and putting what you read in your own words.* This is what he learns about the howler monkey:

1. *It can smell its food — leaves and fruits — more than one mile away.*

2. Its tail can be really long — five times as long as its body in some cases — and the howler monkey can grab stuff with it.

3. It kind of sounds like a bear, and it opens its mouth wide to make it look like a big circle.

Wow! Howler monkeys are so interesting, Richard thinks. He even gets to see a real one and hear it in a video online. Why hadn't he just done his report in the first place? Why did he have to be so dumb? All he'd had to do was tell where they live and why they live there. That would have been so easy. Now he still has the report to give on Friday — looming in front of him. Plus, now he has to give it alone, without his group. Richard shakes his head at himself.

● ● ●

As soon as Richard and his dad walk into the house from the library with the two books, Richard goes straight up the stairs to his room. He can't wait to read up some more on howler monkeys. There's so much to know.

Of course, as soon as he walks into his bedroom, there's Darnell sitting on the floor playing video games. Richard sets his books on his desk and sits down. He opens his notebook and one of the howler monkey books. He goes to the table of contents to see where the stuff about habitat is located.

"Whoa," Darnell calls out.

Richard looks over at him, then turns back to his book.

"Awesome!" Darnell calls out again.

"Darnell, I can't concentrate with all that noise you're making."

"That's not my fault," Darnell says.

"You know I have to get this report done. I have to give the presentation on Friday."

"Too bad, so sad," Darnell says with a big grin on his face. His eyes are fixed on his video game. "You brought all this on — whoa!" He begins to raise his shoulders up and down one at a time — his way of showing he's winning. *Very annoying,* Richard thinks.

"Can you take that somewhere else?"

"No, I can't. This is my room. I have the right to be in my own room." He squints at the small screen.

"Anyway, if Mom sees me, she'll just think of a chore for me to do."

Richard looks out the window. Still raining. He gathers his belongings and goes out the door and down the stairs. The dining room is deserted at the moment. There's usually something happening at the dining room table, but now it's nice and quiet. Roland and Jamal are helping Mr. Robinson, who lives down the street, clean out his attic. His mother is off to the beauty salon and his father is napping on the family-room couch. Richard looks up at the ceiling toward the room above. The only one making noise in the whole house is Darnell with his video game. *That's okay,* Richard thinks. All he has to do is finish the report, make sure his homework is turned in every day, ace the spelling test on Friday, and mind all his p's and all his q's...then he'll be back to playing video games, watching TV, and playing basketball at recess. And going to Gregory Johnson's skateboard party next Saturday.

Nine
P's and Q's

Richard doesn't like seeing his name on the board under the word "Benched." It's just below Calvin Vickers's name. He looks over at Calvin. It's morning journal time, and Calvin looks as though he's struggling with getting something down on paper. He has his tongue between his teeth and his face is scrunched up with effort. The topic for that day is *My Weekend*, which is always the topic on Monday. *That's easy*, Richard thinks. He takes out his journal and begins to write:

I had a good weekend and I had a bad weekend. But the good thing is going to make next Saturday REALLY good. First I was going to be on punishment all weekend and I was going to miss this great party. I was sad about that. But then I woke up and it was raining. That made me so happy. Becuz that party had to be canceled. And now if I'm relly good I can go next Saturday becuz the sun is supposed to shine then and I'll be off my punishment. Plus I'll be able to play video games and watch tv and just do what I want. I'll be happy.

He finishes at the same time he hears Ms. Shelby-Ortiz say, "Okay, everyone, put your journals away. Let's get ready for reading." Sometimes she collects the journals. Sometimes she doesn't. You never know when she's going to have someone go around the room and collect them, like Deja, who snatches the journal right from under your hand. Richard prefers it when Nikki collects them. She's really polite and says things like "You're not finished? Okay, I'll come back to you." Ms. Shelby-Ortiz sometimes likes to look over the journals for spelling errors and run-on sentences and just plain messiness. Then she makes you go to the next clean page and rewrite that day's entry for homework.

Richard looks up at the spelling word list on the big poster paper on the classroom easel. Ms. Shelby-Ortiz always puts the new list up on Mondays so the students can see the words every day until the day of the test. Richard starts to read them and his heart sinks. There are only eight words out of eighteen that he's pretty sure he can spell. There is a whole mess of tricky words with silent letters and two letters making one sound, and then there's *quotient*. The answer to a division problem. Why would anyone have to know how to spell that? *Quotient*.

Richard looks up at the ceiling and tests himself: *q-o-t-s-h* ... He knows that's not right. He takes a peek and sighs. He's way off. How is he going to learn how to spell ten really hard words by Friday? He starts to write down all the *w* words with silent letters, but Ms. Shelby-Ortiz interrupts with instructions for the class to take out their readers and go to their groups. It's a good thing he got a good night's sleep, because other-wise Yolanda Meeker would surely have him keeling over from boredom.

After reading and going back to his desk to complete workbook pages, Richard realizes something. He's getting all his work done in a *timely fashion*. And it hasn't been that hard. All he has to do is remember to focus and not get off track trying to see what others are doing. *Ralph really has that bad,* Richard thinks. Every time Ms. Shelby-Ortiz gives an assignment, he does all this stalling stuff: getting up to sharpen his pencil after breaking the point on purpose, asking questions that Ms. Shelby-Ortiz had gone over two seconds before, claiming he can't find his workbook in his desk. Richard shakes his head slowly just at the thought of it.

When the class is dismissed for recess, Richard walks straight to the row of benches and sits down — away from Calvin Vickers. As Ms. Shelby-Ortiz says, the bench is not a place to talk. The only things you can do on the bench are homework, read a book, and watch the other kids play.

Richard didn't bring out homework or a book, so he busies himself watching the basketball game going on in front of him. Beyond that he sees something he really doesn't want to see: Harper coming his way with a big smile on his face. He plops himself right next to Richard once more. "How's it going? You not playin' again?"

"I'm benched," Richard tries to say while keeping his mouth as closed as possible.

"Say what?"

Harper should know that there's no talking on the bench. Nobody should even be sitting too close to another benched kid. The bench rules are very strict. An infraction could add another day, in fact.

"I'm benched," Richard whispers.

"Oh, man . . . What you do?"

Out of the side of his mouth

and looking straight ahead, Richard says, "I didn't do my project."

"Why not?" Harper asks in a loud voice.

Miss Campbell, the yard lady, keeps looking their way. Harper is going to get him in trouble. "Cuz," he says, hoping this will satisfy Harper's nosiness. "We're not supposed to be talking," he adds, and moves down the bench. Harper scoots down the bench too, until he's right next to Richard again.

"We're not supposed to sit next to each other," Richard says. "We're going to get in trouble."

"So?" Harper says. "I don't care."

Richard looks away and keeps his mouth closed. Harper might be big but he can't make Richard talk.

Apparently tired of Richard being no fun, Harper gets up and heads for the bathroom, seemingly without a thought to Miss Campbell.

Finally the freeze bell rings. After a few moments the second bell sounds and Richard can get up and join his class.

● ● ●

"Harper was trying to get me in trouble," Richard says to Gavin as they walk home. "He was sitting all next to me, which he knows is against the rules, and then he kept talking and trying to get me to talk. He didn't even care that he could get in trouble. He said so."

"Wow," Gavin says. "Wonder why he's like that?"

"That's a good question," Richard says.

● ● ●

By Thursday, Richard is worried. He's been really minding his p's and q's, but he knows that's not going to save him on the spelling test. On Thursdays Ms. Shelby-Ortiz gives the students time to quiz one another in place of journal writing. The good thing is you can work with a buddy. So, after some negotiating with Chi Chi, she moves to Gavin's seat at Table Four and Gavin takes her seat at Table Three.

"Turn your word list over," Gavin says, "and put your workbook over it." Richard does what he says. He's desperate.

"I can spell ten of the words already," Richard says. "Just give me the ones I put a little check by."

"*Quotient*," Gavin says.

"Don't give me that one first. Start with the ones with silent letters."

"*Wrist*," Gavin says.

"*W-r-i-s-t.*"

"*Rough,*" Gavin says.

"Oh, shoot," Richard mutters. He closes his eyes to visualize the word. "Okay, I got it. *R-o-u-g-h.*"

"Right," Gavin says.

"That's not on the list."

"No, I mean you got that one right."

"Okay, give me *quotient.*"

"*Quotient,*" Gavin says.

Richard takes a deep breath. "*Q-o* —"

"No," Gavin interrupts.

"Wait, wait, don't tell me."

"Come on," Gavin says. "*Q-u-o . . .*"

"*Q-u-o,*" Richard begins, and then pauses. "*T-i-e-n-t?*"

"Yes, yes. You got it!" Gavin says. "Now just do that tomorrow."

Richard already knows that. It doesn't matter that he could spell the word for Gavin. He needs to spell the word correctly on the test tomorrow. That word could mean the difference between going to the skateboard party and *not* going to the skateboard party. Everything is riding on that one word.

Richard decides to take his spelling list to the bench at recess. He needs to go over the words he's still a little shaky on. But just as he unfolds the paper with his spelling words, here comes Harper flopping down beside him. "Whatcha got?" Harper asks.

Richard looks over at Mr. Beaumont, the other third grade teacher. He must be filling in for Miss Campbell or something. He's blowing his whistle at two boys at the water fountain who are spitting water at each other. "My spelling words for a test tomorrow."

"Want me to quiz you?"

"No, thanks. I like to quiz myself."

"Let me see them," Harper says, snatching the list out of Richard's hand. He peers down at the words. "Whoa! These are some *hard* words."

"I know most of them," Richard says.

"Let me see. Spell *school*."

"*S-c-h-o-o-l.*"

"Yeah, okay. Now spell *quo*—uh—*quo*—*t*—uh ..."

Richard looks over at Mr. Beaumont, who now has both of the spitters by the shoulders and is marching them over to the benches. Richard takes back his paper and spells *quotient* in his head. He checks the word. Again, he got it right!

Ten
Last Day

The sun is shining brightly when Richard opens his eyes. *A good sign,* he thinks. Darnell is already in the shower, which is unusual, and which means the bathroom is going to be all steamed up when it's Richard's turn. While he's waiting, Richard pulls the spelling list out from under his pillow. For some reason, he thought sleeping on it might help.

There's something about that word — *quotient* — that still has him worried. He doesn't know why. He has no problem with words like *demonstrate* and *electric* and *wrinkle*. He's been spelling *quotient* correctly since yesterday, but somehow he fears that when Ms. Shelby-Ortiz says the word during the spelling test, he'll choke and his mind will go blank.

He looks at his poster for his presentation, which he has been working on all week. It's the first time he's done a project completely alone, without his mother's help.

● ● ●

"How are you feeling?" Richard's mom asks as she passes him the new box of Cinnamon Crunch.

Richard shakes some cereal into his bowl under the watchful eyes of Darnell and Jamal. "I feel okay," he says, then pours some milk into his bowl.

"Think you're going to get a hundred on that spelling test?" she asks.

Richard hesitates, remembering how grim his row of low grades looked in Ms. Shelby-Ortiz's grade book when she angled it on her desk so that his parents could get a good look.

"Ready to give your presentation about the howler monkey's habitat?" she continues

Richard swallows. "Uh-huh." He takes a bite of cereal.

"I'm sure you'll do fine," his mother says.

"If I get a hundred on my spelling test, can I skateboard after school?"

"Not at the park. In front of the house and in the driveway." She's looking for something in her purse. "Where are my keys?"

● ● ●

When Richard enters his classroom, he has butterflies in his stomach. He checks the schedule on the whiteboard. The spelling test is right after morning recess. His presentation is right after lunch. The whole day feels full of stress.

On top of that, at recess Harper won't let him study his words. Richard had taken his time leaving the classroom just so Harper would be settled before Richard got to the benches. But as soon as Richard takes a seat far down one of the benches, Harper scoots over until he's right next to him.

"You still studying them words?" he asks.

Richard looks around for Miss Campbell. He doesn't see her.

"Yeah," Richard says. He wishes Harper would go away.

"What'll happen if you mess up on it?"

"A lot of stuff," Richard says. "So I better study."

Just then, Harper's attention is drawn away. Miss Campbell is marching Ralph Buyer to the benches. He flops down a little ways from Richard, crosses his arms, and pokes out his mouth.

Harper moves down to him. "Hey, whaja do?"

"Nothin'," Ralph says.

Richard looks down at his word list and his eyes land on *quotient*.

● ● ●

"Okay, class, clear your desks and take out a pencil. Head your paper in the upper right corner and number your paper *on every other line,* one to eighteen." Ms. Shelby-Ortiz has to give these instructions every time the class has a spelling test. Richard's eyes follow Casey as she passes out the special spelling-test paper. Finally, she gets to Richard's table. He does just what Ms. Shelby-Ortiz has requested — puts his name and the date in the upper right corner and numbers the paper, one to eighteen, on every *other* line. He doesn't want to be in the group who will still number every line and put just their names in the left corner.

Richard is careful to follow every direction as his heart pounds in his ears.

When he finishes, he sits back and waits.

At last, the test begins. Ms. Shelby-Ortiz says each word clearly. Then she puts the word in a sentence and says the word once more.

"*Wrist*," she says. "I hurt my wrist playing tennis. *Wrist*."

Richard writes *w-r-i-s-t*. He looks at it, certain he's spelled it correctly.

"*School*," Ms. Shelby-Ortiz says. "I'm doing very well in school this year. *School*."

Easy, Richard thinks, and writes it down quickly.

"*Enough*," she says. "I think I've studied enough for my spelling test. *Enough*."

E-n-o-g-h, he writes. He looks at it closely. It doesn't look right. *What's missing?* he wonders. He spells it out silently. The *u*, he realizes. He forgot the *u*. He erases the word and writes *e-n-o-u-g-h*. *Better*, he thinks.

Richard easily spells every word from then on while he waits for Ms. Shelby-Ortiz to say *quotient*.

Finally he hears her say, "Okay, class. Last word. *Quotient.* The answer to a division problem is called a quotient. *Quotient.*"

Richard's hand is shaking a little. He takes a deep breath and writes *q-o-t-i-e-n-t.* He looks at it. He knows it's wrong. The *u* — why does he always forget the *u?* Richard erases the word and starts all over. He writes *q-u-o-t-i-e-n-t.* He looks at it closely. *Yes!* he thinks. He turns his paper face-down, hiding it from prying eyes. *That's it.*

He can't help smiling when Casey comes to his table to collect the papers. He looks around, happy to have the test behind him. But he's not out of the woods yet. There's silent reading while Ms. Shelby-Ortiz corrects the tests. There's waiting for her to call his name and report his score. She calls out only the hundreds. Then of course there's the rainforest presentation right after lunch.

Richard takes out his Sustained Silent Reading book and looks at the title: *Henry Huggins*. He opens the book and begins to read with his ears tuned, ready to hear the sound of Ms. Shelby-Ortiz calling out his name and announcing that he got a hundred on the test. He looks over at her. She's busy shaking her head over a test she's correcting. He feels a sudden surge of fear. What if that's his paper? What if he's wrong about how well he did? What if he misspelled *quotient*?

"Good job, Nikki. One hundred percent."

Richard tries to concentrate on his book. He's reading the same sentence over and over.

"Good job, Erik. Once again."

Richard begins to click his teeth nervously. Noisily too, apparently, because Rosario looks over at him and frowns.

"And Richard, I'm happy to say. Good job."

Richard can't help grinning and looks down, not wanting everyone to see how much it matters to him, how much it is out of the ordinary for him. He draws in a big breath and slowly lets it out.

● ● ●

When Ms. Shelby-Ortiz calls on him after lunch to give his presentation on the howler monkey's habitat, Richard practically skips to the front of the class. Gavin gives him the thumbs-up. But Richard doesn't need it. What he learned about the howler monkey's habitat is really interesting, and he thinks the class will find it interesting, too.

To start, Richard has the visual aids that he did all by himself. He drew the big shape of South America and put in the countries with pencil first, then traced everything in different-colored markers. He found photographs of howler monkeys online and printed them, cut them out, and glued one in each country where howler monkeys are found. Now Richard sticks the poster into the clips on the whiteboard and then gets Ms. Shelby-Ortiz's pointer, which kids are allowed to use when they give reports. It feels good in his hand.

He begins by telling the class all the ways the different habitats (tropical rainforests, evergreen forests, and seasonal deciduous forests) are alike and why the howler monkey likes them so much. Yolanda Meeker's mouth is hanging open a little bit. *A good sign*, Richard thinks. Ralph looks as though he's paying attention. Another good sign. Then Richard tells the class some things about howler monkeys.

"Howler monkeys like to live in the tops of trees so they can eat the leaves up there and some flowers and fruit and stuff. They like to lounge around and not fight with the other monkeys." Now Yolanda's mouth hangs open more and Carlos puts down the rubber band he's been playing with. "Since they live

in the rainforest and people are cutting down the rainforest, they're kind of losing where they live and stuff. And also the baby howler monkey stays on its mother's back because the father howler monkey will kill it."

Yolanda's eyes get big and so do Carlos's and Ralph's.

"So that's my report." Richard takes a little bow, enjoying himself. After all, he got a hundred on his spelling test. "Are there any questions?"

Yolanda's hand creeps up. "Is that true? Does the daddy howler monkey kill the baby howler monkey?"

"Yeah, lots of times. But the mommy howler monkey protects it a lot of times too."

Yolanda seems relieved. Richard looks around for more questions but doesn't see any more raised hands.

"Thank you, Richard, for that interesting report. Very . . . quick and to the point."

With a big sigh, Richard returns to his desk. His week of punishment is over.

Eleven
The Perfect Flat-Ground Ollie

The sun is shining when Richard opens his eyes. The night before, they'd had a little family celebration when he'd showed his parents his 100 percent on his spelling test. And he'd actually been able to show them, which was a miracle because Ms. Shelby-Ortiz usually files the tests in the students' folders. Plus he got to tell his parents about the howler monkey report. His mother let the boys have root beer floats for dessert and didn't even get mad when Darnell kept blowing into his to make extra bubbles. There was more fun when their dad turned on the basketball game and Richard and his brothers crashed all over the family room to watch it.

Richard watches Darnell snoring with his mouth

open. He looks around for something to toss at Darnell but then decides against it. Barefoot, he pads down the stairs and into the kitchen. He listens to the refrigerator hum. The box of Cinnamon Crunch is on top of the refrigerator. He gets it down and shakes some into his hand. He pulls out his pajama shirt pocket and shakes some into there, too. He goes out to the back porch and looks at his skateboard leaning up against the house. It looks sad, as if it could be feeling abandoned. Richard has been so busy this week with his project and his spelling test and minding his p's and q's, he hasn't had any time to practice.

"What are you doing out here in your pajamas?" his mother asks. Richard hadn't heard her step out onto the porch.

"Looking at my skateboard."

"Why?"

"I don't know."

"You need to go upstairs and wash up and get dressed for breakfast."

"Then can I practice something on my skateboard?"

"We'll see."

His mother always says "We'll see" when she means yes but doesn't want to come out and say it.

Darnell is just stirring when Richard throws on his clothes and then practically skips down the stairs to breakfast.

One by one his brothers arrive at the table and stare at him as they shake the last of the cereal into their bowls. *Will I ever live that blob thing down?* he wonders.

"I've got basketball practice," Roland announces. "I said Jamal could come with me and watch."

"And remember, Mom, I'm supposed to help Mrs. Johnson set up at the park for the party. She's going to be picking me up in thirty minutes," Darnell says.

"I know. I've already talked to Mrs. Johnson."

This couldn't be more perfect, Richard thinks. No one to watch him practice. No one to laugh at him when he messes up. He's got a little bit of time between his brothers leaving and Gavin arriving to walk with him to the park. Richard grabs his skateboard and goes into the garage for his crate.

He places the crate in the middle of the driveway, carries his skateboard to the end of the driveway, and jumps on. But just as he gets to the crate, he chickens out. He's never tried jumping over something before. He decides to try again. He knows he needs to come down on the back of the skateboard at the last minute. Oh, and he needs as much speed as possible.

Richard starts again, but just as he gets to the point where he must push down on the back of the skateboard, thoughts of that boy Evan Richardson come to mind. Evan is the boy in Darnell's class who tried to do a flat-ground Ollie over a crate — and broke his arm.

Richard chickens out again. He stands there staring down at the crate. He's not going to do it. He knows he isn't. He feels a little bit disappointed. He pictures himself carrying the crate up to the skateboard park, then placing it on the sidewalk next to the skateboard area with all eyes suddenly turning to him. He pictures himself skateboarding fast to the crate and then sailing over it, to the crowd's oohs and aahs. *How come so many things don't turn out as you picture them?* he wonders.

Richard returns the crate to the garage and carries his skateboard to the end of the driveway to practice his regular flat-ground Ollie. He gives himself a running start. When he gets to the middle of the driveway, he pushes his heel on the back of the skateboard. It elevates. He jumps to land on the board and ride it as it sails a bit before dropping back to the driveway.

Perfect. *Wow*, he thinks. *I'm pretty good.* Gavin can't do that. Darnell can do it only some of the time. Richard bets even Gregory Johnson can't do the flat-ground Ollie as well as he can.

"What are you doing?" Gavin is coming up the driveway with his skateboard under his arm.

"Something." Richard picks up his skateboard.

"You ready?"

"Wait, I have to tell my mom we're walking to the park now."

● ● ●

Gregory's mom has reserved the skateboard park for two hours, so it's all theirs. Richard feels butterflies in his stomach. He's excited at the sight of the streamers in the low branches of the tree that is shading the picnic table. He's excited at the sight of Gregory Johnson's dad cooking hamburgers on the barbecue grill. He's excited at the sight of the bounce house for Gregory Johnson's little cousins — and the picnic table covered with chips and punch and all kinds of cupcakes. He even likes looking at the pile of presents. He searches for the gift his mother bought and wrapped and that Darnell delivered.

"A book?" he remembers saying when his mom told them what "they" had gotten Gregory Johnson.

"A book?" Darnell had repeated, sounding as if he couldn't believe it. "Why a book?"

"It's an atlas," his mother had said. "It's way better than just looking up a map online. Because you can run your finger over the page." She'd looked at them as if she was expecting them to get it, but then shook her head at their blank looks. "He'll love it, eventually," she said.

Now Richard no longer cares that their present to Gregory Johnson is . . . a *book*. All he cares about is doing his flat-ground Ollie perfectly. Already, boys from Darnell's class are sailing up and down the bowls and along the rims. Richard checks the flat run between two bowls. It's occupied by a few older boys — cousins of Gregory Johnson — attempting some really difficult moves: Nollie nerd flips and underflips and fakie frontsides. Some are even succeeding. A whole bunch of boys from Darnell's class have formed an audience on the bleachers. For every successful feat, a cheer goes up.

Richard swallows as he takes his board down to the flat ground. "Where are you going?" Gavin asks.

"Down there," Richard says, pointing to the end of the line of kids waiting to show off their tricks.

"You don't want to do the bowls?"

"Nah. I'm going to try a flat-ground Ollie."

"You know how to do that?"

"Yeah," Richard says casually, though his heart is pounding. He's never had an audience before.

He gets in line behind one of Gregory Johnson's cousins. Too soon, the cousin is up. Richard hears someone say, "Hey, it's Mark Johnson. He's the best!" Then it's as quiet as a golf course. Mark Johnson pushes off fast on his skateboard and does a perfect frosty flip. Richard's heart sinks. How can he follow that?

"Ooooh!" someone cries from the stands.

"Did you see that?" someone else yells.

Loud whooping starts up and seems to go on forever. Finally it dies down and it's time for Richard to do his flat-ground Ollie. He feels like taking his skateboard and walking off, but with all eyes on him, he can't. He'd never live it down.

He pushes off — concentrating on every part of his body. When it's time, he presses down on the back of the board with his heel. The board leaves the ground. He just has to land on it firmly enough not to fall forward. Richard thrusts himself up and comes down solidly, both feet connecting with the board hard. He rides it out without a stumble. He lets out the breath he hadn't realized he'd been holding. He feels as if he's floating with relief. He did it. He didn't falter. There's a little bit of applause behind him, along with Gavin's whoops that sound extra loud against the sparse clapping.

Oh, well, Richard thinks. He doesn't care. He did it! And he didn't fall!

That alone feels great. He picks up his board and climbs the steps to where Gavin is sitting in the bleachers with a big grin on his face. Gavin looks as

though he is actually proud of Richard. And Richard is proud of himself, too. And now he's also hungry. Right on time, it seems, because just then Gregory Johnson's father calls out, "Okay, everybody come and get it!"

Check out the next book in the Carver Chronicles!

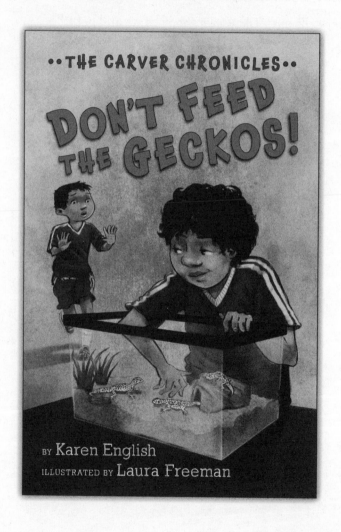

••THE CARVER CHRONICLES••

DON'T FEED THE GECKOS!

BY Karen English

ILLUSTRATED BY Laura Freeman

Carlos's cousin, Bernardo, is coming. It's after school and Carlos sits down at the kitchen table to eat his Toaster Tart and eavesdrop on his mother and Tía Lupe's telephone conversation. His mother and Tía Lupe are always on the phone, checking with each other about everything. At least once or twice a day. His father doesn't even answer the phone anymore because he knows it's probably Tía Lupe.

Carlos overhears that his cousin Bernardo is coming to stay with them all the way from Texas because Bernardo's mom — Tía Emilia — is having a rough time and needs to get a fresh start somewhere else. She's moving to their town and sending Bernardo ahead.

Carlos stops chewing to listen better. Now it sounds as if his mother and Tía Lupe are gossiping about Tía Emilia. She's always having problems; she doesn't make the right choices; she needs to manage her life better; and blah blah blah. Boring grown-up stuff. But it does make him think about his cousin and the fact that he's coming tomorrow.

His mother finally gets off the telephone and comes to sit across from him. She puts on her serious face.

"Now, listen here, Carlos. Do you remember your cousin Bernardo?"

"A little bit." Bernardo was kind of chubby and had a

mop of dark curly hair. Carlos went with Mami and Papi to Texas — San Antonio — before his sister, Issy (short for Isabella), was born. It was Bernardo's birthday; Carlos turned five a few months after him. Carlos remembers sitting on a porch, eating a Popsicle with Bernardo before his birthday party. Oh, and running through the sprinklers. He remembers Bernardo cried because he wanted two pieces of birthday cake on his plate at once. He didn't want to wait until he finished what he had first. He just sat there crying and looking stupid with a mouth full of chewed-up cake.

And Carlos remembers seeing a picture of Bernardo's dad in some kind of uniform — like an army uniform.

"Bernardo and Tía Emilia are moving here. Your *tía* wants him making the change in schools and settled as soon as possible. I'm picking him up tomorrow, so I just want to give you a heads-up."

Maybe this will be a good thing. Maybe Bernardo will be cool and it'll be awesome to have another guy in the house — kind of like a brother. They'll be able to do things together. Mami doesn't let Carlos go to the park by himself, or the store, or anywhere, actually. But with his cousin Bernardo here, he'll have an automatic buddy to go places with. *Yeah,* Carlos says to himself. *Bernardo.*

"What's he like?" Carlos asks.

"How am I supposed to know?" Mami says, sounding a little irritated. "All I know is that you better make your cousin feel at home. Make him feel welcome."

That's important to Mami, Carlos knows. Family. And sticking together and helping each other out.

Now Mami is giving him a list that she's counting out on her fingers — which shows she means business. She still has the serious face where she stares at Carlos, looking at him closely. His little sister comes into the room and stands next to Mami. She's wearing her tiara because she wants to be a queen when she grows up. It's annoying. Ever since Mami told her she was named after Queen Isabella of Spain, she's been wearing that tiara as much as possible. Mami did a report on Queen Isabella in high school, apparently.

"Can I have a Toaster Tart?" Issy asks in a whiny voice.

"Not now, Princess."

"Queen," Issy says. She adjusts her crown. Carlos rolls his eyes.

"Oh, right. *Queen* Isabella. Not now."

Issy must sense that there's something going on that she wants to be a part of. She climbs onto Mami's lap, and then there are the two of them, looking at Carlos like they expect something special from him.

Bernardo has had a hard year, Mami tells him. She

doesn't tell him what that means exactly, but because he has had this hard year, Carlos is to make Bernardo feel extra "at home." Like letting him feed Carlos's geckos. Stuff like that. "And introduce him to your friends, help him in school, share stuff with him."

That sounds super, but Carlos is stuck on letting Bernardo near his geckos. *Uh-uh ... Ain't gonna happen.* At least not without supervision.

Read more about the kids of Carver Elementary in these other great books:

Karen English is a Coretta Scott King Honor Award–winning author who lives in Los Angeles, California. Her books have been praised for their accessible writing, authentic characters, and satisfying story lines.

Karen is a retired elementary school teacher, and she wrote these stories with her students in mind.

Laura Freeman has illustrated several books for children, including the Nikki and Deja series by Karen English. Her artwork has also appeared in publications such as the *New York Times* and *New York* magazine.

Laura grew up in New York City and now lives in Atlanta, Georgia, with her husband and two young sons. Her drawings for this book were inspired by her children, and by her own childhood.